The Footballing Adventures
of
Sidebottom and McPlop

ADRIAN LOBLEY

Children's Books by Adrian Lobley

Humour
The Ridiculous Adventures of Sidebottom and McPlop
The Footballing Adventures of Sidebottom and McPlop

Historical Fiction
Kane and the Mystery of the Missing World Cup
Kane and the Christmas Football Adventure

Educational - Maths
The Football Maths Book
The Football Maths Book - The Rematch!
The Football Maths Book - The Christmas Match
The Football Maths Book - The Birthday Party
The Football Maths Book - The World Cup

Educational - Reading
A Learn to Read Book - The Football Match
A Learn to Read Book - The Tennis Match

For Sebastian

First published in 2019

ACKNOWLEDGMENTS

With thanks to Sebastian Wraith-Lobley

Cover and illustrations by Peter Hudspith

1

The Cup Quarter-final

"Penalty!" One of McPlop's teammates yelled. McPlop had just been sent flying by a defender's tackle right on the edge of the penalty area and was sent soaring into the air.

"That's got to be a penalty!" Screamed one of his other teammates.

McPlop meanwhile was still mid-air and was now rapidly plunging towards the ground. The penalty area wasn't so much grass, more mud. In fact, there was barely a blade of grass to be seen. As McPlop stared downwards to where he was about to land, a large puddle of mud came into view, which he was rapidly heading for.

"Uh oh." He muttered.

SPLATT!

"OOOooo." Said some of the other players as they watched their plump teammate McPlop splash down in the muddiest puddle on the pitch.

"That's got to be a penalty ref!" Yelled a man on the sidelines. The man was leaping up and down hysterically and waving his arms around. It was Sidebottom and it was his team.

"Let me just check your player's okay before I make a decision." The referee shouted over to Sidebottom.

"Stuff the player! No one cares about McPlop." Sidebottom yelled back. "That's a penalty!"

Meanwhile McPlop, who was in some pain, gingerly lifted himself up. As he extracted himself from the mud it made a SHLURPP sound.

"He's going to be okay," announced the referee.

"No one cares!" Shouted Sidebottom from the other side of the pitch. "That has to be a penalty."

"I need to consult with my linesman to see if it was a penalty." The referee explained to everyone in earshot.

Sidebottom was barely able to contain himself by now on the touchline. He had only recently created his new team, Sidebottom United and they had now reached the heady heights of the quarter-final of the local 'Bob Poppleton Bakery Cup'. In Sidebottom's head, this was a huge, huge match.

The referee wandered over to where the linesman was standing. The linesman was just a man who had been out walking with his son when the referee asked him if he would hold a linesman's flag and wave it if he saw a foul of any kind. The only problem was that the man had been paying no attention at all when McPlop had been hacked down, as he had been tying his son's shoelaces.

The referee reached the linesman and then pretended to have a conversation with him. The twenty two players watched on bemused as the referee then put his hand to his ear as though he was listening to something.

"Does he think he has a small radio in his ear and is listening to what the other linesman is saying?" Asked one of the players, to a teammate standing next to him. The teammate looked over to the other linesman who was also paying no attention.

Meanwhile McPlop had waddled back to his teammates who were now congregated together just outside the penalty area. They were looking a bit bored.

Only five local teams had entered the cup and as Sidebottom United were a new team, they and one other team had to play a 'quarter-final' to establish which team joined the other three in the semi-finals.

"Don't you realise how important this is?" Screamed Sidebottom at the referee. "This is the Bob Poppleton Bakery Cup quarter-final! And that was a penalty!"

The referee suddenly started running back to the penalty area, stretched his arm out in the direction of the penalty spot as he ran and blew his whistle.

"Yessss!!" Shouted Sidebottom punching the air. "He's given a penalty!" The manager looked over at the linesman.

"Well done linesman! Brilliant decision!"

The linesman looked back at Sidebottom blankly as he hadn't actually said anything to the referee other than, "I didn't see it."

The Sidebottom United players were standing in a circle.

"So, who's going to take the penalty?" Said one of them. They all looked at each other blankly. Then suddenly the chubby frame of McPlop barged between two of the players.

"I, the great McPlop, will take the penalty." He announced. "I was once voted the thirty sixth best penalty taker in Division Six of the Garforth League." He explained proudly.

McPlop picked up the ball, put it under his arm and walked towards the penalty spot and placed it down.

Sidebottom saw McPlop step back to take the penalty and realised he needed to show his management authority.

"McPlop," he shouted, "you take the penalty. I want you to take it. You're the main man. You're my assigned penalty taker."

McPlop was now feeling very happy and supremely confident. He had taken a number of steps back, spread his legs and stuck out his chest. He pulled his shorts up extra high so that they were almost under his armpits. All the players watched as McPlop did a bizarre run up on his tip-toes, towards the penalty spot. As McPlop went to boot the ball as hard as he could though, he slipped just as he was about to strike it. He caught the edge of the ball and sent it slicing off to the right. It had missed the goal by a long distance and now seemed to be heading towards the corner flag.

"McPlop you idiot!!" Shouted Sidebottom. "I told you not to take the penalty!"

The ball eventually trickled over the white line at the side of the pitch.

"That didn't even go for a goal kick!" Exclaimed Sidebottom. "It's gone for a throw in! How is that even possible,

McPlop!" Sidebottom was jumping up and down like a madman.

Just then the referee blew his whistle to end the first half. All the Sidebottom United players trudged over to the manager for their team talk. Sidebottom handed the players a couple of plates of sliced oranges and the team started tucking into them.

"That's good men, eat some of that healthy fruit. The score's still 0-0, so this match is ours for the taking," said the manager.

McPlop however wandered past everyone to the burger van parked behind them.

"Hello sir, what can I get you?" Asked the burger van man as McPlop approached the counter.

"I've only got a couple of minutes as it's half-time so I'll just have a double cheese burger, with a milkshake and fries."

"Right away sir,"

"And some extra fries on top of the normal fries."

"Extra fries as well, yes sir."

"And three doughnuts."

"Three doughnuts too. No problem."

Within a minute McPlop had walked back to his teammates, his arms full of food and a double cheeseburger stuffed in his mouth.

"Ijurrrneeededaquicccckksnarrr"

"What??" Said Sidebottom. "McPlop, take that burger out of your mouth, I can't hear a word you're saying."

The other players had finished their half time oranges and were starting to wander back onto the pitch ready for the second half to start.

"Urr, McPlop, you do realise there's a football match going on here, that you're supposed to playing in." Sidebottom pointed out.

"Yurrrr." Said McPlop chomping on his next big piece of burger. He plumped himself down on a chair that was by the edge of the pitch and watched as the opposition players made their way on to the football field.

"Oh, yes, do have a seat, McPlop." Sidebottom commented sarcastically, "There's no rush. There's only twenty one other players and the referee waiting for you to finish your burger."

"Won't be long." McPlop stuffed some fries in his mouth and washed it down with some of his chocolate milkshake. Sidebottom watched as some of the milkshake spilt down the front of McPlop's football top.

"For goodness sake." Sidebottom muttered.

All twenty one players and the referee were now standing watching McPlop.

"In your own time, McPlop," said his manager, tapping his watch, "don't you rush your meal on account of us."

McPlop nodded his head and stuffed a doughnut in his mouth.

"I do have a meeting I need to attend at work tomorrow though, so if you could finish your three course meal by then, that would be useful," added Sidebottom.

The referee was getting annoyed too.

"Oi, 'Doughnut Boy', how long are you going to be? We need to kick off!"

McPlop peered into the bag in front of him.

"Shouldn't be long, just got two more doughnuts left."

The referee tutted. He then blew his whistle to start the second half without McPlop.

"Get up, McPlop!" Screamed Sidebottom. "He's started without you. We're down to ten men you idiot."

McPlop shoved the last of his doughnuts into his mouth, wiped his sugar coated hands on his shirt, which was now covered in sugar, ketchup and chocolate milkshake, and trundled onto the pitch.

"Just stay up front out of the way, McPlop," ordered Sidebottom.

McPlop looked back round, let out a huge burp in his manager's direction and then wandered up front.

Twenty minutes on and there were still no goals. Sidebottom on the touchline decided to try and start a chant amongst the crowd of three people standing near him.

"U-ni-ted! U-ni-ted!"

The crowd of three people looked at him skeptically.

"Mexican wave!" He shouted at the three of them and then suddenly jumped out of his seat and threw his hands up in the air.

The trio took another cursory look at him and then went back to their conversation.

Sidebottom went back to concentrating on the match. The opposition were now pounding the Sidebottom United goal. The keeper somehow tipped a shot onto the bar. There was a desperate scramble to get it clear but the ball got played back into the middle. The opposition striker hit it sweetly on the volley and the ball shot towards the goal. The Sidebottom United keeper stood motionless, watching as the ball hit the inside of his post and went across the face of the goal and away from danger.

"Phew," said Sidebottom on the touchline.

More time passed and still the score was deadlocked at 0-0. The opposition were all in the Sidebottom United half and were blasting shot after shot at the goal but somehow hadn't managed to score.

There were only a couple of minutes left.

After one great save by the keeper, the ball fell kindly to one of the Sidebottom United fullbacks. He looked up the field and could see only one of his teammates in the opposition half. It was McPlop. He groaned. There was no one else in space. The opposition players had left McPlop on his own as they had assumed, quite correctly, that he didn't really need marking.

The opposition players were now closing in on the Sidebottom United full back, who still had the ball at his feet. He didn't have much time. So, he put his foot through the ball and launched it as far as he could upfield yelling 'McPlop!' at the top of his voice.

McPlop, who had been daydreaming and wondering whether, if he nipped off the pitch for thirty seconds to buy another doughnut, anyone would notice, suddenly heard his name being shouted. He then saw the ball sail over his head and land in front of him.

McPlop shuffled as fast as he could after the ball to try and reach it before the opposition goalkeeper, who was coming in the opposite direction, straight towards him.

All the other players had seen what had happened and were now turning and sprinting to get back. McPlop had a huge head start but was so slow that everyone was catching up with him.

McPlop was nearly there though. Just as he reached the ball, everyone else had caught up. He stuck out a boot and toe-punted the ball towards the goal. The goalkeeper managed to get in the way and the ball deflected off him and ran out for a corner. Sidebottom groaned on the sideline.

"My grandma could have scored that, McPlop!" He shouted.

All the Sidebottom United players came up for the corner. There was less than a minute left on the referee's watch and it was still 0-0. They were gambling everything on it and had left no one in defence.

The Sidebottom United winger had jogged over to the corner flag, placed the ball down and was now about to run up and cross the ball in.

McPlop meanwhile had noticed what he thought was a piece of doughnut on the pitch near where he was standing on the penalty spot. As the corner came in McPlop had bent over, with his backside facing the opponent's goal, to pick up the piece of doughnut.

Incredibly all the other players missed the ball and it thumped against McPlop's huge backside and went thundering towards the top corner of the goal.

Everyone stood and gawped as they watched the flight of the ball.

It hit the post and incredibly went in!

McPlop turned around just in time to see the ball nestling in the back of the net.

"Yessssss!!" He shouted.

"McPlop you big-butted genius!!!" Yelled Sidebottom on the touchline, as he leapt up and down and tried to give an old lady next to him a big sloppy kiss.

"Full-time." Shouted the referee and blew his whistle four times to signal the end of the match.

"We've won!" Shouted one of the Sidebottom United players.

"We're into the semi-final of the Bob Poppleton Bakery Cup!" Screamed Sidebottom. "It doesn't get bigger than this!"

"McPlop's done it!" Shouted one of his teammates.

McPlop stripped off his shirt and started swinging it around above his head whilst running around and around in circles. He then dived, belly first onto the grass. All his teammates mobbed him.

Sidebottom came running over and dived on top of the bodies. Within a couple of minutes, the players were all celebrating by throwing McPlop up into the air and catching him and then throwing him up into the air and catching him again.

"Hurray for McPlop's backside!" Shouted one of the players. "Hip hip, Hooray!"

2

McPlop Takes The Glory

It was around eight o'clock in the morning on a Sunday and I had just plucked the newspaper from my letter box and was opening it as I walked over to my kitchen table and sat down.

"I wonder what's happening in the local news." I muttered to myself as I scanned the pages. There wasn't much going on, so I turned to the sports pages at the back and was stunned to see a headline about someone I knew. It read:

McPlop blasts Sidebottom United into cup semi-final!

"McPlop? Ha." I said to myself. "How on earth is McPlop the hero? I've seen him play, he's useless."

Just then the doorbell rang. I took a quick sip of tea and made my way to the door.

"McPlop!" I grinned as I opened the

front door. "Or should I call you 'Ronaldo McPlop', the cup hero?" I said, raising an eyebrow. McPlop beamed with pride at my made-up nickname.

"Yes it is I, Ronaldo Messi Pele McPlop." He said excitedly. Just then Sidebottom wandered up alongside him.

"Don't get too cocky, McPlop." Said Sidebottom who had now reached my front doorstep. "It's ridiculous, Mr Langley. I'm the manager who clearly masterminded the whole victory, and this idiot," he pointed his thumb in McPlop's direction, "gets all the glory. All the newspaper headlines. The whole thing's a conspiracy. All the newspaper companies are in on it."

"Good to see you're not paranoid then, Sidebottom." I chuckled. "What have you got there, McPlop?" I said, looking at a cardboard box down by McPlop's feet.

"Oh, he's been to the newsagent," Sidebottom interjected, "and has bought every copy they had of the local newspaper that had his name in it. He keeps banging on that he's now a local celebrity. Every time we come across someone in the street he hands them one of his newspapers and asks them if they want his autograph." Sidebottom shook his head. "They all think he's a madman."

"Ah but what about that lady we bumped into who wanted a selfie taken with me, asked for my autograph and said I was the greatest." Said Ronaldo Messi Pele McPlop.

"That was your mum!" Said Sidebottom in despair.

"McPlop, just one question," I said as I looked McPlop up and down."

"Yes, Mr Langley."

"You're covered in mud and in your football gear, yet it's only eight o'clock in the morning. Why?"

"Ah, yes, I slept in my football kit, after my famous victory yesterday." McPlop replied and nodded his head very knowledgeably.

"It wasn't YOUR famous victory, McPlop!" Yelled Sidebottom. "It's my team!"

"Either way, Mr Langley," continued McPlop, "following my brilliant strike yesterday I decided I would never take off my football kit and never wash again, in order to preserve the moment forever."

"Oh, for goodness sake." Said Sidebottom, rolling his eyes. "Any more of this rubbish and I'm dropping you for the semi-final, McPlop."

"Impossible, Sidebottom!" McPlop exclaimed. "The fans would go crazy if you did that. There'd be rioting!"

"He makes a good point there Sidebottom," I responded sarcastically, "we don't want to see all three fans rioting."

"Plus," continued McPlop, "can you imagine what the press would write in their newspapers if you dropped your star striker, the great McPlop, and then didn't win your semi-final."

Sidebottom frowned as he considered this scenario. McPlop didn't stop there. "The crowd would be chanting

'Sidebottom out'." Sidebottom started looking a little worried. "Imagine if you then got sacked from your own team." Suggested McPlop who was now quite enjoying winding Sidebottom up. "I can see the headlines now: *Sidebottom sacked from Sidebottom Utd as side hits the bottom*." I tried not to chuckle as I listened to McPlop. "You would be laughed out of town, Sidebutt." Said McPlop. Sidebottom was thinking very hard about the potential headlines and pondering what to do.

"Do you know what, McPlop?" said the manager, drumming his fingers on his chin, "I've considered all the possible strategies about the upcoming semi-final and my brilliant tactical brain tells me to stick with the same team. So that means, I'm going to give you one more chance. This is your big shot though McPlop so you'd better do well. There aren't many players that get to play in a Bob Poppleton Bakery Cup semi-final. I'm giving you your launchpad to possible stardom."

"A good decision, Sidebottom." I said and smiled at McPlop who smiled back at me. "So this winning goal of yours, McPlop, was it a good goal?" I asked.

"Mr Langley, it was brilliant! If only you could have been there to see it, the way I finished the goal off from a corner to take us through to the semis was fantastic."

"It was complete fluke!" Moaned Sidebottom throwing his hands up in the air, "it deflected in off your gigantic backside!"

"Don't you take any notice, Mr Langley, the finish was no fluke," explained McPlop as he nodded his head slowly, "I used my left butt-cheek to steer that ball past the goalkeeper. It was precision."

"You were bending over to pick up some doughnut, McPlop you buffoon." Said Sidebottom, who was so red faced he looked like he was going to explode. "You weren't even watching the corner being taken!"

"Ignore him, Mr Langley," replied

McPlop, "it says here in the newspaper that the goal was voted the 27th most curious goal in the Bob Poppleton Bakery Cup, since records began three years ago."

"Oh, I give up." Said Sidebottom. "Right, I have to go as I need to pick up the merchandise."

"What merchandise?" I asked, slightly intrigued at what Sidebottom was up to.

"For the semi-final, Mr Langley. It's not every day you reach the Bob Poppleton Bakery cup semi-final, so I'm having some commemorative mugs made. On one side of the mug there will be a picture of me holding up the Bob Poppleton Bakery Cup trophy."

"And on the other side of the mug?" I asked.

"Ah, another picture of me, this time drinking champagne out of the trophy."

"Hang on a minute, Sidebottom," interjected McPlop, "the other side of the mug should have a picture of your star striker scoring the winning goal from the quarter-final."

"Oh right, McPlop," Sidebottom retorted, "yes let's have a picture of the ball deflecting off your bum on the side of the mug. That'll be nice for everyone. Can you imagine old Mrs Johnson down the road, going to have a cup of tea and every time she goes to dip a biscuit in her tea all she can see is a picture of your backside." Sidebottom shook his head. "That will be really nice for her, I'm sure."

"So how many commemorative mugs are you thinking of having made then, Sidebottom?"

"I was thinking of getting about a thousand, Mr Langley."

"You are aware, that you only have about three fans though? So that would leave you with about nine hundred and ninety-seven unsold mugs."

"Ah well, I've had a brilliant marketing idea, Mr Langley, that will guarantee we distribute more mugs. Firstly, we give them away for free and secondly I get some Sidebottom United scarves made and each person gets a free scarf as well!"

Sidebottom seemed pretty chuffed at this brilliant idea.

"An inspired plan, Sidebottom," I replied, "I can't see how that can fail." I chuckled.

"Plus, it's only going to cost me five thousand pounds for the mugs and another five thousand pounds for the scarves. It's a bargain, Mr Langley!"

"Complete bargain, Sidebottom." I nodded.

"In fact, I can't wait. I'm going to go right now and get them ordered. Come on, McPlop." Sidebottom pulled at McPlop's shirt and the pair of them scurried off to go and blow all Sidebottom's spare cash on his latest insane plan.

3

A Round of Golf

I was sitting in my back garden enjoying the peace and quiet when I could hear someone banging loudly on my front door.

"Who is it now?" I sighed. "I don't get a minute's peace these days." I got up from my chair and wandered round the side of the house.

"Hi, Mr Langley!" Said the two visitors in unison.

"Sidebottom, McPlop. I might have known." I looked at Sidebottom, who was wearing some baggy pantaloons. "Whyyy, Sidebottom?" I asked, gesturing towards his stupid trousers.

"Well, as you know, McPlop and I are practically football professionals now, Mr Langley. I'm already one of the greatest managers ever and McPlop here, is one of the top 'below-average' strikers in the local area." McPlop nodded proudly.

"So what have those ridiculous pantaloons got to do with football?" I asked.

"Well, what do all professional footballers do on their days off, Mr Langley?"

"I've no idea, Sidebottom." I said, rapidly losing the will to live.

"They play golf, Mr Langley. They have so much spare time in between matches they play lots of golf." Sidebottom beamed. "This is my golfing outfit." He pointed down at his insanely wide trousers. "What's more, McPlop and I suspect that we will be brilliant golfers and we wondered if you fancied a game today? We could certainly teach you a thing or two about golf, now that we're football experts."

"Yes Sidebottom, I'm sure that having managed one football match will immediately make you an expert in a totally different sport. I believe that is exactly how it works." I said sarcastically.

"Glad you agree, Mr Langley." Sidebottom replied with glee, totally missing the tone of my voice. "We've also got our new friend coming to play a round of golf with us."

"You've got a new friend, Sidebottom? Well done."

"Yes, he's half Italian and half English."

"What's he called?"

"Francesco Piddle." Sidebottom replied. "He's a bit naughty though. Tends to get into a bit of trouble."

"Really? That should be interesting at the golf club as they don't like people misbehaving." I thought about Sidebottom's offer to play golf with them. "This could actually be quite entertaining. Okay, I'll join you for a game."

"Brutal!" Shouted Sidebottom and punched the air. "I'll see you at my place in ten minutes."

Not long after I had joined Sidebottom and McPlop, we had climbed into Sidebottom's small car. We were now sitting in his driveway waiting for Francesco Piddle to arrive.

"Morning gents." Piddle said as he wandered up to the car. He looked at the battered old vehicle which had both front wings missing and different coloured body parts. "What a piece of junk." Piddle muttered to himself as he looked at one of the doors which was hanging off its hinges.

"Check out my new wheels, Francesco." Sidebottom said proudly as he got out of the mini, to let his friend into the back seat. "She's got a beefed up engine and a mega sound system."

"Is there any chance that we will make it to the golf club alive in this old wreck?" Piddle asked.

"Definitely!" Sidebottom patted the wing mirror proudly, which promptly broke off, crashed to the floor and smashed into pieces. "Don't worry about that, Francesco, I never look in the mirrors anyway. I won't miss it." Sidebottom kicked the pieces of broken wing mirror into his flowerbed. Francesco Piddle frowned at the driver who was still holding the door open for him. He warily climbed into the back seat to sit next to McPlop.

"Mr Langley, this is Francesco Piddle. Francesco, this is Mr Langley. You already know McPlop of course." Sidebottom said, introducing us.

"Morning, Piddle." I said and shook hands with him.

"We're off!" Announced Sidebottom before I had finished the handshake. He slammed the car into reverse and rocketed backwards out of the driveway without actually looking to see if any cars were coming. I grabbed my seat belt and clicked it into place as quickly as I could, as we roared down the road.

After twenty minutes we could see the golf club coming into view. A cloud of exhaust fumes trailed after the car.

"We're here!" Sidebottom said excitedly. He bombed the little car round the bend into the golf club entrance as we all clung on for our lives. We could smell the burning rubber from the tyres as the car screeched round the corner. The car was almost on two wheels now and close to tipping over. There was a sign that read, 'Please drive slowly'.

"What did that sign say?" Shouted Sidebottom as we whizzed past it. "I was going too fast to read it."

"Never mind that, watch out, Sidebottom!" I yelled as the momentum of the car carried it towards the pavement and straight for another sign. The car bounced up onto the pavement. The sign read, 'Please drive carefully.' Sidebottom was desperately trying to keep the vehicle under control but was losing the battle. The front of the car smashed into the sign and disintegrated it. Sidebottom managed to grapple back control and brought the car to a skidding halt in the middle of the car park. We all breathed a sigh of relief.

"How cool was that!" Shouted the driver.

He then leapt out of the car and headed over to the golf clubhouse. The three of us climbed out of the car and trailed after him, happy to still be in one piece. Sidebottom had already reached the desk.

"Can I help you, sir?" The lady behind the desk asked, smiling. Sidebottom clicked his fingers at her.

"Four of your finest golf clubs please, my good woman." He said. The woman raised her eyebrows, very unimpressed by the way Sidebottom had spoken to her and glared at him. She then reached into a large box behind the counter, fished her hand around in it, picked out the worst four clubs she could find and handed them over to him. We had reached the desk by this time.

"Let's head for the first tee." Sidebottom said to us as he strode away from the desk, towards the golf course.

"Sidebottom," I said, "we can't play golf with one club each. The clubs she's given us are all putters as well. They're only any use when we get the ball onto the green and need to putt the ball into the hole. We need other clubs such as a Driver, Iron and Sand Wedge for when we're on other parts of the course."

"No need for a sandwich Mr Langley, had one before I came out."

I groaned.

"Not a 'sandwich', you buffoon. A 'Sand Wedge'. It's a club that you use when the ball goes into the sand bunker.

"I'll just use my trusty old putter here, Mr Langley." Sidebottom waved around the rusty club which looked as though it was going to snap at any time. I am so good at golf I can hit a three hundred yard drive using just this putter."

I shook my head in resignation, wondering why I had actually come along today. I looked around and noticed that only McPlop was with us.

"Um, Sidebottom. Where's your new friend?"

"Francesco Piddle?"

"Yes."

"I overheard him mention something

about getting us a golf cart. You know the ones, they're like a tiny car with a motor in them so you can drive down the golf course." McPlop commented.

"That would at least save us having to walk." I replied.

Just then a horn sounded. We turned round to see where the sound was coming from, namely behind a long bush near the first tee. Then all of a sudden a golf cart came crashing through the bush and was heading straight for us.

"I've got us a golf cart, lads!" Shouted Francesco Piddle in a strong Yorkshire accent, as he careered towards us at a rapid pace. We all dived out of the way. The four putters got abandoned and the cart rode straight over them, snapping Sidebottom's rusty putter in half.

"My putter!"

"Well that'll put an end to your three hundred yard drives, Sidebottom." I commented as I picked myself up off the floor.

Meanwhile Francesco Piddle yanked the

handbrake on and turned the wheel sharply. The golf cart skidded round with the back wheel locking and cutting up the grass. A huge lump of grass and mud flew up leaving a big hole gouged out of the golf course.

"Check out the wheels, lads!" Piddle said excitedly. "Did you see that skid stop?" Piddle then took off the handbrake, turned the car round and slammed his foot on the accelerator. The cart had a powerful motor and the wheels started spinning as it tried to rocket off. The beautifully manicured green grass started spewing up into the air with the mud below it churning up and flying off behind the cart. It was carnage. Just then the president of the golf club came out of the pavilion to see what all the commotion was.

"Oi! You there!" He shouted in a very posh accent, pointing at Piddle in the golf cart. "What the devil do you think you're doing?"

Meanwhile Piddle was wondering what

other mischief he could get up to. He looked round onto the back seat of the cart and saw there were some golf clubs.

"Yo Preso!" He shouted back up the golf course to the president of the club, who was now fuming. "Here's one of your golf clubs back." Francesco Piddle then slung one of the clubs straight up into the air out of the golf cart. It cartwheeled over and over and then landed on the fairway behind, taking another divot out of the grass.

"I have never seen behavior like this at my club before!" Screamed the president who was now very red-faced. He stormed back into the pavilion to try and get some help.

"Hey lads," I said to Sidebottom and McPlop, "fancy a bit of fun?"

"Like what, Mr Langley?" McPlop asked, as we all watched Francesco Piddle launching the other golf clubs out of the golf cart and laughing hysterically.

"Don't forget your other golf clubs, Mr President." Piddle shouted.

"Well," I said, watching Piddle bomb down the fairway, "how about we grab those clubs Piddle has thrown out of the cart and see how good our aim is?" I jogged down the fairway picked up the clubs and returned to the tee and passed Sidebottom and McPlop a club each.

"Watch this." I said, as I placed my golf ball on the tee and then swung my club back. I brought it through, striking the ball perfectly. The ball flew down the fairway right in the direction of Piddle and his golf cart.

"Direct hit!" I shouted. The ball struck the back of the golf cart. Piddle, who was still driving the cart, almost leapt out of his skin.

"What was that!" He exclaimed as my golf ball put a big dent in the back of the cart.

"Ha, my turn now," said Sidebottom, having seen what I had done. He whacked his ball as hard as he could in the direction of the cart.

Piddle had worked out what we were

doing, so was now weaving all over the golf course to make himself a more difficult target. He was now using it as an excuse to drive through as many of the flower beds as he could. Flowers and mud were churning up everywhere.

"What do we do now?" Asked McPlop, after he had whacked his golf ball towards Piddle's cart.

"Let's get ourselves a golf cart and follow Piddle!" Yelped an excited Sidebottom who was now jumping up and down. He ran around the corner. After a few moments the same bush beside us got flattened again as Sidebottom crashed through it in another golf cart that he had swiped from somewhere.

"Aargh!" Shouted McPlop, who had to dive out of the way to avoid being run over.

"Jump in!" Shouted Sidebottom, as he slammed the brake on the cart and dug up a huge lump of grass out of the golf course. McPlop got up and nodded appreciatively at the cart.

"Nice wheels, Sidebottom." He commented. "How much did you have to pay for these?"

"Urr, never mind that, McPlop. Get in! Let's catch up with Piddle!"

Neither McPlop or I fancied waiting around for the club president to come back out and start shouting at us, so we jumped into the cart. The instant our bums landed on the seats, Sidebottom slammed his foot hard on the accelerator and the cart started churning up more of the turf before shooting down the fairway after Francesco Piddle.

"Woo hoo!" Shouted Sidebottom with his head out of the side of the cart. After a minute or so we had almost caught up with Piddle who was now driving round and round in circles trying to get the cart to tip over onto its side.

"Watch out, Sidebottom!" I yelled as we headed straight for Piddle who was now on two wheels as the cart was almost tipping over. Sidebottom swerved to try and avoid him but only succeeded in crashing into him and diverting our cart off towards one of the small lakes. Meanwhile Piddle's cart had completely turned over and was now upside down on its roof. Piddle climbed out, laughing.

"What a result!" He shouted, punching the air. Piddle looked up to see Sidebottom's cart, with myself and McPlop on board, careering towards the lake.

"Not the water!" I shouted. Sidebottom had frozen though and wasn't responding to my pleas. We were only twenty metres away and zooming at high speed towards the lake. I grabbed the steering wheel from Sidebottom and at the same time pulled the hand brake on as hard as I could. The cart skidded round with McPlop and I desperately clinging on to the cart. Sidebottom however wasn't holding onto anything and as there were no doors on the cart, as we spun round to a sharp halt, Sidebottom went flying out of the side of the vehicle, straight towards the lake. He bounced down the side of the banking and made a huge splash as he entered the water.

McPlop and I couldn't stop laughing.

Francesco wandered up and stood beside us, watching as Sidebottom trudged out of the small lake, dripping wet and covered in green algae.

"I think it might be time for us to go." I commented as I heard some shouts from the direction of the clubhouse, "I think the president's coming down to tell us off." I set off in the opposite direction. "Everyone, come this way, I know a short cut that'll take us to the car park." We wandered back past the upside down golf cart and ducked through the trees at the opposite side of the fairway.

"That was brilliant," said McPlop, "I hadn't realized how much fun golf is! Please can we come again, Mr Langley?"

"We can but we might have to come in disguise next time as I doubt they would let us in after we've destroyed half of their golf club." I said grinning.

We all clambered into Sidebottom's

poor excuse for a car and headed for home.

4

A New Referee

I had decided to go for an early morning jog around the local village and having run up a sweat, I sprinted the final fifty metres up the road towards my house. Turning the corner I rounded my hedge and ran down my driveway. I was confronted by a very familiar sight.

"Mr Langley!" Shouted an animated Sidebottom, who was standing outside my front porch with McPlop. "It's an emergency!"

"What's an emergency?" I asked, panting and slightly worried. "What on earth's happened?"

"It's the big match today," explained Sidebottom, "and we don't have a referee. The man who was supposed to referee the match has phoned me to say that his rabbit has caught a cold and he needs to buy some rabbit medicine from the vets, so that will rule him out for most of the day."

"Sounds like a rather flimsy excuse." I commented.

"It's a disaster, Mr Langley. It's the Bob Poppleton Bakery Cup semi-final today!"

I just shrugged my shoulders at this piece of fairly irrelevant news.

"It's huge, Mr Langley. My team, Sidebottom United, have a chance of reaching the final!"

I shrugged my shoulders again.

"So, what do you want me for?" I queried.

"Well, we know you used to be a referee so we thought you might referee the match, Mr Langley!" McPlop nodded as Sidebottom spoke. "You'll be handsomely rewarded," Sidebottom explained, "Bob Poppleton says that his bakery company will provide a day's worth of free bread to anyone who offers to referee the match." Sidebottom looked impressed at this offer. "That's the equivalent of one whole loaf of bread, Mr Langley! For free!"

"Well, there's no denying that getting one whole loaf of bread for free is tempting, Sidebottom." I replied. "It would bring the cost of my weekly shop down from £68.75 to £68.00. I'd have to work out what on earth I was going to do with the huge pile of cash that I'd have saved. A holiday perhaps. New car maybe."

Sidebottom was nodding furiously.

"So you'll do it, Mr Langley?" He asked.

"Tell Poppleton, he can keep his bread." I smiled. "I don't mind refereeing the game."

"He shoots! He scores!" Shouted McPlop, who was as excited about the news as his manager was and started punching the air.

"Steady on, McPlop." I said.

"We'll see you at 2:30pm on the bottom pitch, Mr Langley. We're playing in red. The opposition are called, 'Team

Awesome' and are in blue."

"I'll dig out my whistle and red and yellow cards, especially for the occasion."

"Brutal!" Shouted Sidebottom. "Come on, McPlop, let's go and tell the other players."

The pair shot up my driveway and disappeared round the corner. I shook my head and smiled as I opened my front door and wandered into the house.

I arrived at Sidebottom United's ground dressed in my black referee's kit and wandered over to the pavilion. I opened the door and stepped past loads of football boots that were lined up behind it. I could smell the familiar football changing room aroma as soon as I entered.

On the right as I walked down the corridor was the home team changing room so I knocked and entered.

"Afternoon, lads." I said. As I scanned the room I only recognised one person other than Sidebottom and McPlop. It was the mischievous, Francesco, who I had heard from Sidebottom was a great midfielder.

"Afternoon ref!" Francesco shouted.

"Piddle." I said, nodding my head to acknowledge him. I turned to address all the players.

"Now, I want a fair game, lads. No dangerous tackles and no talking back to me. Any misbehavior and I get the yellow cards out and book you."

Just then Francesco Piddle wandered over to the door that lead out to the pitch and just started booting it, for seemingly no reason whatsoever. Everyone turned and watched him. He kept on kicking the door. Everyone looked a little bemused.

"Um, Piddle," I said, "what do you think you're doing?"

"You can't book me," Piddle replied, "I'm not on the pitch."

"Good point, Piddle. You keep kicking the door then." I shook my head, turned round and wandered back out of the changing room. Sidebottom darted out after me.

"Mr Langley, have you heard about the graffiti epidemic?" He asked.

"What graffiti epidemic?"

"Look over here." Sidebottom took me further along the corridor and pointed out all the writing that was scrawled on the wall.

The first words read, *'Sidebottom's a wazzock'* followed by, *'Piddle is the greatest!'* with another one that read, *'McPlop is a carrot-chewing donkey!'*

"Interestingly it's all written in the same handwriting, Mr Langley but I can't work out who wrote it." Sidebottom said, scratching his chin.

"Might I suggest that you speak to Piddle about it." I said raising an eyebrow.

"Ah, you think Piddle might know the person who wrote it?"

"I'm pretty sure Piddle knows exactly who wrote it." I replied, rolling my eyes. "You might want to check whether he happens to have a black marker pen in his bag too."

"Ah! I understand now."

"Good."

"Someone must have written all this stuff on the wall with a black marker pen," concluded Sidebottom, "and then put the pen into Piddle's bag!" He looked very pleased with himself for thinking he had figured out the mystery.

"I can literally feel my life drain away, Sidebottom." I muttered. "Right, I have a match to referee, so I'll see you in a bit." I marched out of the building and headed for the pitch.

Sidebottom meanwhile returned to the dressing room and coughed to announce his arrival. A hush fell over the room as everyone waited for the manager to speak.

"Lads, this is a very special moment. It's not every day you reach the Bob Poppleton Bakery Cup semi-final. So, to mark the occasion I have a present for each of you."

There was a slightly excited murmur from the room in anticipation of what it might be.

He opened the box by his feet and passed each player a commemorative mug.

Francesco Piddle looked at the mug he had been passed, turned it around in his hand to examine both sides, each of which had pictures of Sidebottom on. A big bin with a black bin liner in it was right next to Piddle so without looking he chucked the mug over his shoulder and it landed in the bin. As there was no other rubbish in the bin though, it hit the bottom and smashed.

"What was that?" Exclaimed Sidebottom. Everyone shrugged including Piddle who put on his most innocent expression.

"Can I have one of those commemorative mugs." Piddle asked.

"I could have sworn I had just gave you one." Sidebottom replied, a little confused.

"No, I've definitely not had one." Lied the mischievous Piddle.

"Okay, here you go." Sidebottom

passed Francesco another mug before continuing to hand out a few more to other players who had just arrived.

Piddle analysed the mug he had been handed, saw that Sidebottom wasn't looking and then chucked the mug over his shoulder. It landed in the same bin behind him and smashed as soon as it hit the bottom.

"What was that!" Said Sidebottom, spinning around. Piddle pointed up at the open window.

"Think it was the kids outside, Sidey. You know what they're like around here, always throwing glass milk bottles about. Kids will be kids."

"Ah, that's a relief, I thought one of my mugs had been broken."

Piddle shook his head.

"Definitely not, Sidey. By the way, my girlfriend said that she really wanted one of your commemorative mugs for her birthday. She asked me if she could have one."

"But how did she know about the

mugs, Francesco?" Sidebottom looked confused. "I've only just told you about them." Piddle ignored his question.

"She's a huge Sidebottom United fan and told me she thought you were the best manager in the league." When Sidebottom heard this great news he stood up straight and stuck his chest out.

"Well, I can certainly believe that." He nodded. The manager reached into his box of mugs and passed Francesco another one. "Here you are, would she like me to sign it? She probably will."

"Go for it!" Said Francesco, who delved into his bag and handed Sidebottom a black marker pen.

Sidebottom scribbled his name on the mug and handed it over to Francesco Piddle.

"Cheers, Sidey." Piddle replied.

Piddle waited until Sidebottom looked away, then chucked the latest mug over his shoulder. It flipped over and landed plum in the middle of the bin and smashed into pieces as soon as it hit the bottom.

"Right! Time for the match." Piddle stated, as he stood up quickly and slapped a confused looking Sidebottom on the shoulder on the way out of the changing room.

"Those pesky kids, Sidey. I'll go and have a word with them. We won't have any milk bottles left at this rate."

5

The Cup Semi-Final

About thirty minutes after the manager had handed out his mugs and free scarves, the eleven Sidebottom United players were on the pitch along with their opponents, Team Awesome, ready to kick off. I looked over at Sidebottom on the touchline. He appeared to be dipping a paint brush into a can of white paint and then painting a large rectangle around himself. I wandered over just as he had finished.

"Sidebottom, we're about to kick off. What are you doing?"

"Painting my technical area, Mr Langley. The managers on TV all have a technical area." He beamed.

I watched as the expression on his face suddenly dropped and changed to a huge frown as he looked past me.

He was now glaring at a couple of doddery old ladies, who were walking very close to his newly painted technical area.

"No one else is allowed inside this technical area except the Sidebottom United manager." Sidebottom announced very loudly in the direction of the old ladies who were now getting really close to his technical area and paying absolutely no attention whatsoever to what he was saying.

I watched as one of the ladies walked over the corner of the white painted rectangle.

"Stop." Said Sidebottom, to them and held his hand up to make a stop sign. "Do you know anything about football techniques?" Sidebottom asked one of the ladies politely.

"No, young man." She replied.

"Then get out of the technical area!" He shouted.

"Well, I've never been spoken to so rudely!" The old lady said and whacked Sidebottom with her handbag.

"Ouch!" Sidebottom exclaimed and dived to the ground. "Referee, did you see that!" He shouted as he rolled over three times. "That's got to be a yellow card."

I watched as Sidebottom rolled over his newly painted white lines and got paint all over his back.

I had seen enough. I turned around and blew my whistle to start the game.

Sidebottom United had won the toss and were about to kick off. McPlop stood with one foot on the ball. At the sound of the whistle he passed it back to one of the midfielders. It was Piddle. Piddle ran with the ball at the opposition. He skillfully dribbled past one player, then another, then a third.

Sidebottom had now finished his premier-league roll on the floor and realising that he wasn't going to be able to get the old granny booked, started shouting out advice.

"Shoot, Piddle, shoot!" Piddle ignored

him and dribbled past a fourth player and was now heading towards the opposition penalty area.

"Shoooottt!" Sidebottom screamed.

Piddle was already getting annoyed by Sidebottom shouting instructions at him, so suddenly stopped. Everyone else stopped. Piddle then booted the ball as hard as he could off the pitch and straight into the river that ran alongside the football field.

Sidebottom stood and gawped.

"That's our only ball." Sidebottom said, who was the nearest person to the river. "I'd better go in and get it." He concluded.

Sidebottom jumped into the river and waded through it. It went right up to his armpits. He fished the ball out and threw it back onto the pitch. As play got underway, the manager clambered up the riverbank, dripping wet.

After another twenty minutes it was still goalless but the opposition were dominating possession and the Sidebottom United goal was taking a pounding. Their opponents had hit the crossbar twice so far. Then, just outside the area, the Team Awesome striker was doing lots of stepovers to try and fool Piddle as to which way he was going. Piddle was getting very wound up as he tried to block his way and watched the striker jinking in one direction, then another but not actually moving anywhere.

"Get stuck into him, Francesco!" Shouted Sidebottom from the sidelines. Francesco Piddle didn't need telling twice. He booted the opposition striker right in the goolies.

"OOOooo," The player groaned as he crumpled to the ground. Piddle saw that the ball was now available and started dribbling it upfield.

I blew my whistle, loudly. "Free kick!" I shouted. "Get back here, Piddle."

"For what referee?" Piddle shouted back. "I barely touched the man." The poor opposition player was still on the floor.

"You booted him in his private parts!" Yelled one of the player's teammates.

"He dived." Replied Piddle dismissively.

"I'm giving you a warning this time, Francesco. Anymore of this and I'll book you." I said as I strode over. Piddle pretended to be helpful and passed the ball back to the opposition player but 'accidentally' kicked it too hard. It bounced off the player who was just getting up.

"Ouch."

The Team Awesome captain, who was called Dave Pants, helped his player stand and gave Piddle a glare. He then placed the ball on the ground just outside the penalty area, ready for his free kick. The Sidebottom United goalkeeper got into position as Pants ran up to the ball. He curled it around the makeshift Sidebottom United wall. The ball rocketed at speed and squeezed just between the goalpost and the despairing dive of the goalkeeper.

"Yesss!" Shouted the Team Awesome players as they all hugged the captain, Dave Pants.

Sidebottom was furious.

"That was your fault, Francesco!" He yelled from the touchline. "Why are you kicking him in the peanuts on the edge of our area? If you need to kick him in the peanuts, do it further up the pitch!"

Piddle had heard enough from Sidebottom, so he grabbed the football from one of his own players. He then dropped it to the ground, took a run up and booted the ball in Sidebottom's direction. It landed with a splash in the river not far from the manager.

"Not again!" Sidebottom moaned. "I'm only just drying off from last time."

A few minutes later, a soaked Sidebottom trudged back to his technical area, with play on the pitch having resumed.

As the clock ticked on, eventually I blew the whistle for half-time with the score reading:

Sidebottom United 0-1 Team Awesome (Dave Pants)

The Sidebottom United players wandered over towards Sidebottom's technical area. The manager walked to the front of his rectangular box to make sure none of the players crossed his white line.

As they gathered before him he looked into his bag to find his tactics board, only to realise it wasn't there.

"Blast, I've left my whiteboard in the car. Right, you lot, wait here. I need to nip to my car and get it. I'll be two minutes."

The players all watched Sidebottom run off. Piddle stood with his hands on his hips examining the big white painted rectangle on the ground in front of him. He then wandered over to the pot of white paint.

"What's he up to?" Whispered McPlop out of the side of his mouth, to the player next to him.

"I think he might be planning on altering Sidebottom's technical area." The other player said, grinning.

Piddle meanwhile had picked up the pot of paint and the brush and was now in the process of drawing a large triangle along the top of Sidebottom's rectangle.

"What's the triangle for, Francesco?" Asked McPlop.

"That's the roof." Responded Piddle, as he added some more detail and then walked to the bottom of the rectangle and started drawing a door.

"Ha. A house." Laughed, McPlop. "He's even drawn a little chimney with smoke." McPlop shook his head. "Sidebottom will do his nut, when he sees this." Piddle put the finishing touches to the door and then stood back to admire his handiwork.

He then wandered over to one side of the rectangle and drew a three dimensional table with a cereal bowl on it. Piddle then put the paint tin and the brush back where he had taken them from and returned to sit down in what used to be the manager's technical area.

Just then Sidebottom came running around the corner carrying his white board and a bag of red and blue counters. He came to a sudden halt as he arrived at the white painted lines. His face dropped in shock, as he saw all the new lines everywhere and a grinning Francesco Piddle sitting on the grass inside what used to be his technical area.

"What on earth is this?!" Sidebottom exclaimed.

"It's my new house." Explained Francesco, who was sitting between the painted door and the painted three dimensional table. He gave his manager his biggest grin. "Do you like it?"

"What on earth do you think you're doing, Francesco?"

Francesco looked around at the table with the painted cereal bowl on it.

"I'm about to eat my imaginary Weetabix." Francesco explained.

"Weetabix!" Exclaimed Sidebottom as he watched Piddle pretend to scoop a spoon into the cereal bowl and eat his Weetabix.

"Have you quite finished now?" Sidebottom said in his best headmaster's voice.

"Well, I wouldn't mind a round of toast as well." Piddle said as he looked round. "Although I'd have to paint an imaginary toaster first though."

"Get out of my technical area!!" Screamed Sidebottom.

"Suit, yourself." Said Piddle, as he stood up deliberately slowly and wandered over to the painted door. He pretended to open the door and then pull it to a close, behind him. Sidebottom glared at him.

At about this time, I blew the whistle for the second half and all the players came jogging back onto the pitch. Sidebottom meanwhile was furiously drawing another technical area further along from Piddle's new house.

About ten minutes later Sidebottom

United were experiencing an unusual period of dominance. Having forced the opposition keeper into two saves in the last couple of minutes, there was another attack beginning.

The Sidebottom United right winger beat two players out by the touchline and then curled a beautiful cross into the box. The ball went over the centreback's head, straight to McPlop. The striker saw the ball was arriving at just above waist height, so he decided to attempt a flying scissor kick.

Using all his strength to lift his heavy frame off the ground, McPlop swung his foot around his body and connected with the ball. The ball however went in completely the wrong direction and went sailing off the side of the pitch. Everyone watched as the ball landed with a splash in the river.

"Not again!" Shouted an irate Sidebottom. "I'm not getting it this time!" He yelled. McPlop felt a bit embarrassed at how bad his shot was.

"It's okay, it was my fault." He said, as he waddled off towards the water. When he got to the small riverbank he took off his shoes and then decided to do a huge belly flop into the water. The ball and half the contents of the river splashed up into the air and out onto the banking.

Just then a man and his dog came wandering along. The dog had seen McPlop diving into the river and thinking that it looked like a lot of fun, ran away from its owner and leapt into the water.

"Nooo!" Shouted the dog owner. "My dog can't swim well." He saw McPlop, who was still in the water. "Please can you get my dog!"

"Of course." Said McPlop who managed to grab the small dog, who was struggling to keep his head above the water. He helped it up the banking and away to safety. A man with a camera who had been hanging around, took a photo of McPlop and then disappeared. McPlop took no notice and climbed after the dog and sat down on the grass to put his boots back on.

"Thank you very much, sir." The dog's owner said, as he pulled a lead out of his pocket and clipped it onto the dog's collar. "He's normally so well behaved and doesn't run off."

"No problem at all." Smiled McPlop, who put his soaking wet feet into his football boots and then shuffled back onto the pitch.

The match was whizzing by with only twenty minutes left on the clock when Francesco Piddle picked up the ball from the half-way line. He proceeded to slalom past four Team Awesome players and entered the penalty box. He was one on one with the keeper with two defenders heading towards him.

Could he do it?

Could Piddle get the crucial equalizer?

Calmly Piddle slotted the ball between the keeper's legs and shouted, "Megs," as he wheeled away in celebration, as the ball ended its journey in the back of the Team Awesome net.

It was 1-1 !

Piddle couldn't contain his excitement and ran off towards the corner flag to celebrate. As he approached the wooden pole and flag, he booted it as hard as he could. The pole, with flag attached, went flying out of the ground and then Piddle picked it up and hurled it, like a javelin, into the river.

He then turned back to the players, who were all looking a little confused, punched both fists in the air and shouted, "That's what I think of your corner flag, Team Awesome!"

"That's our corner flag, Piddle, you idiot!" Shouted Sidebottom. "We're at home!" Sidebottom was shaking his head with despair. "Twenty quid that's going to cost me, Francesco, for goodness sake."

"Ah, sorry, Sidey." Said Francesco, who was now calming down a little. "Worth twenty quid though, to see that goal." He winked at his manager, who just tutted.

The players got the game underway and

the match looked like it was going into extra time, when in the last minute the Sidebottom right winger picked up the ball on the edge of the opposition box and drilled in another brilliant cross. It evaded all the players until Francesco Piddle slid in at the back post. He got the end of his boot to it and somehow managed to steer the ball past the goalkeeper's flailing glove.

"Goooooooooooooooooaaaallllllll!" Sidebottom yelled, trying to keep the word going as long as his breath would allow him, in the mistaken belief that he was now a Brazillian commentator celebrating a World Cup final winner.

He then looked up to see Francesco heading off towards the other corner flag to celebrate.

"Not my other corner flag, Francesco!"

Sidebottom could see another twenty pounds about to vanish into the river.

As Piddle approached the corner flag he held his arms aloft, celebrating. Much to Sidebottom's relief he carried on running past the corner flag. However, he kept on running, still with his arms up.

"Where's he going?" Said McPlop, to one of his teammates.

"Not sure. He seems to think he's running towards the crowd to celebrate, except that there's no crowd."

They watched as Francesco kept running and running, still with his arms aloft, until he ran into the next field. Where he kept on running. He then ran through that field, still celebrating, until eventually he vanished from sight.

All the other players looked at each other, a little bemused.

As there were only a few seconds left I decided to blow my whistle to signal the end of the match, with Piddle's goal the last action of the game.

"Yessss, we won 2-1!" Shouted the Sidebottom United players as they all hugged each other.

Sidebottom came charging onto the pitch.

"We've done it, we're through to the final! I'm a genius!" He shouted as he leapt up and down like an excited lamb bounding towards its mother.

Final Score:
Sidebottom United 2-1 Team Awesome
(Francesco Piddle 2)   (Dave Pants 1)

Man of the match: Francesco Piddle

6

Transfer News

It was early morning on the day after the Bakery Cup Semi-final and I had a satisfied feeling as I sat down at my breakfast table to eat my Frosties.

"Yes, a job well done." I muttered to myself as I thought about how I had performed as referee the previous day.

At that point I heard the letter box on my front door open and then snap shut and the newspaper land on the floor.

"Ah, the local rag." I said to myself and wandered through to the hallway to pick up the paper. "I wonder if Sidebottom will get the headlines?" I muttered. "Or perhaps it will be all about that crazy Francesco Piddle for getting both goals."

I turned the newspaper over to look at the football section on the back page. The headline read: *Hero McPlop, rescues dog from certain death.* There was a picture, so big that it covered most of the page, of McPlop rescuing the dog from the river.

"Ah, the chap who took the photograph of McPlop when he was rescuing the dog must have been a photographer from the local newspaper." I concluded.

Below the headline the article told how Sidebottom United's star striker, McPlop, had thought nothing of his own safety and had dived into the river to save the dog.

"Ha! There's not even a mention of Sidebottom." I chuckled to myself. "He'll be furious when he reads this."

It was later on in the afternoon when the phone rang in McPlop's house.

"Top Bins! Someone's calling me." McPlop was very excited as he didn't receive many calls. He answered the phone with his best telephone voice.

"This is the McPlop residence. McPlop speaking."

"Ah, hello. Is that the same McPlop

who rescued a dog from drowning in the river yesterday?"

"Yes, it is I, the hero, McPlop."

"Good. I'm ringing from the local radio station. I wondered if we could interview you live on the radio to talk about your heroics."

"Certainly!" McPlop pushed out his chest with pride. "I, McPlop, am at your service."

"Excellent. Please can you come down to the radio station in the centre of town at three o'clock tomorrow."

"Definitely. I will see you there." McPlop placed his retro phone back into its cradle and sat down to bask in his own glory.

At three o'clock the following day McPlop had arrived at the building which housed the local radio station. He was now seated in a little booth with the local radio DJ and had just placed some headphones over his ears as he had been told to. The DJ pointed at the red light above the door to show McPlop that they were now live on air and that all the radio listeners would be tuning into their conversation.

"Good morning everyone. This is DJ Brown and I'm delighted to say we have with us today, our local hero and Sidebottom United star striker: McPlop."

"Hi there, viewers." Said McPlop and waved his hand furiously at the DJ.

"Ah, there are no viewers. Just listeners because this is radio, so they can't see you waving." Explained the DJ. McPlop put his hand down, as DJ Brown continued. "So tell us about the rescue then…"

"Well, DJ Brown, there was a huge river with waves as high as houses, crashing into the river bank. All the sail boats were smashing into the side banking and no one dared go anywhere near the river. The dog was drowning, but with no concern for my own safety, I dived in." The DJ raised his eyebrows at hearing McPlop's description of the incident but let him continue anyway. "It wasn't just any dive though Mr DJ sir…."

"No? What kind of dive was it?" Asked the DJ.

"Well, have you seen people jumping off diving boards at the Olympics and they get marks out of 10 from different judges, so a competitors score might be 7.5, 7.5, 7.0, 8.0, 7.5?"

"Yes. I've seen that. If they hardly make a splash then they get really high marks."

"Exactly. Well, I can tell you that the dive I did was a 10.0, 10.0, 10.0, 10.0, 10.0."

"Very good. I think at this point, before you continue your story, we can go to telephone line 4 where we have a caller who wants to ask you something." The DJ pressed a button in front of him. "Hi caller, I understand your name is…" The DJ checked a piece of paper that had just been handed to him. "Mr P.Iddle. Hello, Mr Iddle. What would you like to say to our hero of the hour?"

"Well, it's nothing to do with the dog

rescue. It's a football related question. I would just like to ask McPlop what he thought about the rumours that he is due to be sold by Sidebottom United today."

"Well, that's very interesting news." Said DJ Brown. "Mr McPlop, I didn't know anything about this, do you have any response to the suggestion that you might be sold?"

"Pah, Sidebottom United wouldn't sell me. I'm their star striker."

"I'll have to break you off there Mr McPlop because we have another caller on line 3." The DJ looked at the piece of paper he had just been passed. "It's a…Mr Sidebottom. Well, well, well, this could be the manager of Sidebottom United himself. Perhaps he will be able to shed some light on this exclusive transfer news." The DJ flicked a switch. "Good afternoon, Mr Sidebottom."

"Good afternoon, DJ Brown."

"We heard from a caller, Mr P.Iddle, that there are rumours you are going to off-load your star striker, McPlop, who we actually have here in the studio."

"Well," said Sidebottom, "just this morning the club has received a firm offer for McPlop from Spawn United."

"Spawn United!" Interrupted McPlop. "They're rubbish!" Spluttered the star striker into the microphone.

"They've made a very tempting offer though, McPlop." Explained Sidebottom.

"How much? One million pounds? Two million pounds?" Shouted McPlop. DJ Brown seemed a little surprised at McPlop's valuation of himself considering he had only played two matches in a bakery cup competition.

"It was a very, very tempting offer that gave me little choice." Sidebottom commented.

"How much?!" Shouted a now frantic McPlop.

"Two tracksuits."

"What?"

"Two tracksuits." Sidebottom repeated. "They've offered us two tracksuits in exchange for you."

"Two tracksuits! Is that all?"

"And an apple pie."

"An apple pie!"

"Yes, it was very nice." Sidebottom was rubbing his stomach.

"So you've already sold me then?!" McPlop blurted the words out.

"Well," said Sidebottom, who was now looking at himself in his hallway mirror, "lets just say that I'm currently wearing a nice new top of the range Kappa tracksuit."

"What?" McPlop was furious.

"Yes. I've even got a spare one, if you're short."

McPlop sat there in silence, unable to take in that he had been sold.

"Well," said the DJ, who had now ended the call from Sidebottom, "that was the Sidebottom United manager, delivering a huge bombshell. Mr McPlop, do you have any comment?"

"I can't believe," whimpered McPlop quietly, "that all I'm worth is two tracksuits."

"And an apple pie, don't forget." Pointed out the DJ, trying to lift McPlop's spirits a little. "Sounded like it was a tasty one as well."

An hour later, a fed up McPlop was trudging home and saw me at my kitchen window doing some washing up. I gave him a nod of acknowledgement and that was enough for him to turn into my driveway and head for my front door. I dried my hands on a towel, hung the towel on its peg and went to open the door.

"Mr Langley, some terrible news." McPlop mumbled.

"I heard, McPlop. I was listening in on the radio."

"I think there might be a chance that I might not make it as a premier league footballer now."

"Really?" I replied, a little surprised that at thirty two years of age McPlop was deluded enough to think he could make it to the big time.

"Yes. There was a rumour that scouts

from Real Madrid and Barcelona were going to be at the Bob Poppleton Bakery Cup Final. I could have been snapped up, Mr Langley."

"Really?" I raised my eyebrows. "Probably a bit unlikely though I would have thought."

"I wouldn't have gone cheaply though, Mr Langley. I would have created an auction for myself between Real and Barca so they would fight to get me and I would then demand a multi-million pound wage package."

"Sounds fair." I said with a chuckle.

"But now it won't happen as I'm no longer a Sidebottom United player." McPlop moaned.

"Actually, McPlop, I might have some good news for you."

"What's that, Mr Langley?" McPlop's face brightened a little. "Have you had a call from Real Madrid about me?"

"Urr. No."

"Oh."

"Do you know who Sidebottom United

are due to play against in the final of the Bakery Cup?"

"No, the other semi-final was being played earlier today. I don't know the result yet."

"Well, I can tell you that, Spawn United won 1-0 and are through to the final to play Sidebottom United!"

"Spawn United!" Exclaimed McPlop.

"Indeed."

"But I play for them now." He spluttered. "I've just signed for them! They just bought me for two tracksuits."

"And an apple pie." I added.

"So, I'll be playing against Sidebottom's team?"

"You will indeed!"

"This is huge." McPlop was now doing a little jig up and down. "Imagine if the Barcelona and Real Madrid scouts spot me!" McPlop punched the air. "I'm back in the game, Mr Langley!"

"Indeed. They're probably preparing a contract for you as we speak." I suggested.

"Top bins." Commented McPlop with a smile and a slow nod of his head. "They might whisk me off to Spain on a private jet straight after the final, Mr Langley."

"Definitely." I said, shaking my head in disbelief at the whole conversation.

"I'm going to go home straight away and start learning to speak Spanish."

"A brilliant idea, McPlop." My visitor then paused and frowned as a thought entered his head.

"The only problem though, Mr Langley, is that if I move to Spain, you won't get to see me as I will be in a whole different country."

"Don't forget, we get La Liga matches over here in Britain, McPlop. So I can just switch on the television to see you playing for Real Madrid any time I like."

"A good point, Mr Langley. Phew." McPlop was nodding his head, delighted that we had come up with a solution to his latest problem.

"If I score a goal, I'll lift up my shirt and under it will be another shirt that reads, "I've scored Mr Langley!"

"Again. Another inspired idea, McPlop."

"Right, I'd better go and fish out my passport, Mr Langley." And with that, McPlop turned and sprinted up the driveway and off into the distance.

7

The Gaming Session

McPlop's grandfather clock had just chimed ten o'clock in the morning and McPlop was on his first floor landing jogging on the spot whilst doing lots of bizarre hand stretching exercises. He was particularly excited as Sidebottom was due to turn up at his house at any moment for one of their Playstation Fifa sessions. It was always an epic battle and he was pumped up for it. McPlop shouted to his voice-activated music system which he had programed to be called "Eric".

"Eric. Play motivational music!" The machine pumped out "Eye of the Tiger" from his favourite boxing movie, "Rocky".

McPlop, who was wearing a head band, string vest and some shorts, started running furiously on the spot and punched his fists out in front of him pretending to box against an imaginary opponent.

"Take that Sidebottom!" He shouted, picturing Sidebottom in front of him. "Your computer players are going to get obliterated!"

Just then, the doorbell rang.

"Brutal! He's here." McPlop had been waiting all week for their latest session which was likely to last all day and most of the night. He bounded down the stairs two at a time and flung the door open. Sidebottom was standing there beaming, just as excited about the marathon session.

"McPlop, your computer men are about to get their butts kicked!" Sidebottom declared, as he stood on McPlop's front doorstep, with his specialised blinged-up controller in his hand.

"Pah. Bring it on, Sidebottom." McPlop stepped aside to let his opponent in.

"Which room?"

"You're in bedroom 1 and I'm in bedroom 2." Replied McPlop. "We'll play a network game. We're in different rooms as I'm not having you copying my tactics and seeing my formation." McPlop explained.

"Ha! Your formation?" Laughed Sidebottom. "Last time instead of a 4-4-2, you played a 2-1-7 formation and accidentally put your goalkeeper up front."

"At least he scored." Countered McPlop.

"Yeah, into his own goal!"

"Never mind that, I've been practicing. Those computer pixels of yours are going to get thrashed."

"Yeah, yeah, yeah." Replied Sidebottom and moved his hand to mimic a person's mouth opening and closing repeatedly.

The pair disappeared upstairs and with McPlop having already set the game up, they launched straight into it.

"Baggsy be Newcastle United." Yelled Sidebottom from Bedroom 1.

"I'll be Manchester United, then." McPlop replied.

"You'd better not have rigged this system to cheat in your favour, McPlop."

"Silence Sidebottom, you buffoon. Concentrate on getting your useless players ready for the first match."

A few minutes passed and the pair were ready to play their opening fixture.

"Who are you playing against?" Asked Sidebottom about McPlop's Manchester United team.

"We're at home against Watford."

"Watford!" Sidebottom groaned. "How easy is that! We're away at Arsenal. I knew you'd rig the game so that it gave you the easier fixtures."

"It's a league, doofus!" Exclaimed McPlop from his room. "We have to play all the same teams!"

"Yeah, yeah. I see you're playing at home as well. Might have known. I bet you've programmed a 'cheat' into the system somehow that means all you matches are at home and mine are all away from home."

"Hit the play button, you big jessie!"

Yelled McPlop. "We'll never get to play a game at this rate, with all your insane conspiracy theories."

Sidebottom did his hand movement again mimicking McPlop's mouth opening and closing repeatedly, whilst waggling his head.

"I can see that!" Shouted McPlop, who couldn't see Sidebottom's hand movement as he was in the other bedroom but knew Sidebottom would be doing it.

A few hours passed and the title race was hotting up with Newcastle United and Manchester United level at the top of the league.

"It's the big match!" Announced McPlop from Bedroom 2, as he looked at the next fixture which was Newcastle United versus Manchester United. "Prepare to be destroyed, Sidebuttocks!"

"Ha, by your team of losers? No chance."

The two bedrooms were next to each other just off the first floor landing. As there was a wall opposite, McPlop picked up a ball that was next to him and threw it hard at the landing wall at a diagonal angle. The ball bounced off the wall straight into bedroom 1 where Sidebottom was perched over his screen analysing his team's tactics. The ball whacked him on the head.

"Oy!" He shouted.

McPlop punched the air. "He shoots, he scores! What a rebound! You've got to admire the genius of that rebound Sidebottom," McPlop commented, "I couldn't even see where it was going."

"It's lucky for you that I sold you from Sidebottom United, McPlop, otherwise I'd have dropped you for that."

"Ha. You only get accuracy like that when you're a Spawn United player, Sidebottom. You'll learn about that when you manage a decent team."

McPlop leaned back in his gaming chair as the Newcastle United v Manchester United match kicked off on the screen in front of him. "This is pressure, Sidebottom. Everything rides on this match." McPlop opened a mini-fridge at the side of him, pulled out a plate of doughnuts and started munching his way through them nervously.

"Come on!" Sidebottom screamed at the computer pixels on the screen in front of him.

"Your pixels are going down, Sidebottom." Yelled McPlop.

"They're not. We're massacring you. You've barely got out of your own half!" Countered Sidebottom.

The match went on and was still 0-0 after about seventy minutes. At that point Sidebottom's Newcastle United winger crossed the ball over and his striker did a flying scissor kick. He made a perfect connection with the ball and it rocketed into the top corner of McPlop's team's net.

"Yesssssss!" Shouted Sidebottom and leapt out of his chair thumping the air. He danced out into the hallway and into the doorway of bedroom 2 where McPlop was slumped in his chair, distraught at his team conceding.

"1-0, 1-0, 1-0, 1-0." Chanted Sidebottom as he continued his little jig up and down in McPlop's doorway. McPlop was getting wound up. He picked up a fully loaded Nerf gun from the table next to him and aimed it at Sidebottom.

"Eat this, sucker!" Shouted McPlop and blasted six rubber bullets in Sidebottom's direction – rat-a-tat-tat. Sidebottom dived out of the way and then scrambled back into his room.

McPlop meanwhile rubbed his chin as he pondered his situation.

"Hmmm, this isn't good." McPlop muttered to himself. He then thought of something, raised an eyebrow and grinned mischievously. "Time to get a little help." He said to himself.

McPlop, who was particularly good at computing, had been on the internet the day before and had found a way of triggering some 'cheats' in the computer game which would give him an advantage over Sidebottom. He now clicked a button and a message popped up that read, 'Would you like to apply the 'Red Card' cheat?'

"Ha, time to cause old Sidebutt a few problems." McPlop sniggered. He hit the 'Yes' button.

The match restarted with Sidebottom winning 1-0. McPlop's winger was now attacking and Sidebottom pushed the button forward on his fancy controller to make a tackle. The man he was controlling missed the player and the ball completely. However, McPlop's computer winger dived to the ground and started rolling around holding his leg for no reason whatsoever.

"What on earth!" Shouted Sidebottom. "I didn't touch him. That was a dive, referee!" He screamed at the computer referee on the screen before him. The ref blew his whistle and marched over.

"Good decision ref!" McPlop offered from the other room. "That was a disgraceful foul!" He chuckled. "Your players are all hooligans, Sidebottom.

That's got to be a red card." He shouted.

"You stay out of this, McPlop. This ref's an idiot."

The next thing Sidebottom saw was the referee pulling out a red card.

"A red card!" Screamed Sidebottom. "He didn't even touch him!"

"Well done, referee!" McPlop laughed. McPlop could hear Sidebottom getting out of his chair and coming round.

McPlop clicked another button on his screen and a message appeared that asked the question, 'Cancel the 'Red Card' code cheat?' McPlop hastily clicked the 'Yes' button and the message disappeared from the screen. Sidebottom appeared in his doorway and before McPlop had chance to pick up his nerf gun to blast him, Sidebottom was over and peering at his screen to see if he could spot anything that McPlop might have been up to.

"You'd better not have installed a 'cheat' program, McPlop."

"Sidebottom, you're invading my personal space. Buzz off back to your own room." McPlop said. Sidebottom ignored him and frowned with concentration as he looked at McPlop's screen. He was sure McPlop was up to something but couldn't see any obvious evidence. He stormed back into bedroom 1 and sat down in the cheap gaming chair that McPlop had got for him from an old jumble sale.

"Rats. Now that I've lost one of my defenders, I'm going to have to bring on my last sub to shore up my defence." Sidebottom muttered to himself.

"You might want to bring on your last sub to shore up your defence, Sidey." Shouted McPlop from the other room, grinning.

"Yes, very good. Thank you McPlop. If I wanted your help I'd ask for it."

"Just trying to help a friend out." McPlop said with an innocent a voice as he could.

"I'm still winning 1-0 remember and there's only twenty minutes left." Sidebottom shouted from the other room.

McPlop frowned. In amongst all the fun he had forgotten he was still losing. "Time to get a bit more help I think." He muttered to himself. He then clicked another button and a message came up with the following question, 'Would you like to apply the 'Increase player rating' cheat?'

McPlop hit the 'Yes' button and he was then presented with a list of his Manchester United players and was asked to select one. McPlop chose his worst striker, who had a Fifa rating of 68.

'Enter new rating for this player.' Instructed the console. McPlop changed the number from 68 to 98 and then clicked the 'Done' button. The player's rating immediately changed to 98.

"What's taking so long in there, McPlop, get on with it!" Yelled Sidebottom.

"Just doing a substitution, Sidey. Don't get your knickers in a twist." McPlop brought his new 98 rated striker onto the pitch and hit the 'Continue' button.

"Finally!" Complained Sidebottom. He recognised the player coming on. "Brought your useless reserve on I see, McPlop." Sidebottom said smugly, totally unaware of the players new Fifa rating.

"Button it, Sidebottom."

The game kicked off again. Within a few minutes McPlop's 98-rated striker had picked up the ball. He went on a slaloming run, dribbling past four of Sidebottom's players. Sidebottom couldn't believe it. None of his players could keep up. Then the striker shot and the ball rocketed past the keeper and into the back of the net.

"Yesssss!" Screamed McPlop. He jumped out of his seat and shot round to Sidebottom's doorway and started pointing and singing at Sidebottom. "You're not singing, you're not singing, you're not singing en-ee-more, yorrrrr not sing-ing en-nee-more." He did a little dance and made his hand into an 'L' for Loser sign and put it up against his forehead.

Sidebottom reached down onto the floor, picked up the ball that McPlop had hit him with earlier and then launched it at McPlop. McPlop jumped back out of the way and returned to his room, chuckling.

Sidebottom cancelled the replays and kicked the game off, just as McPlop had sat back down in his luxury gaming chair. The game continued for another few minutes without incident. Then all of a sudden, McPlop's 98-rated player started another weaving run. Past one player, then a second, then a third. McPlop then pressed to chip the ball and the little player lobbed the ball over the opposition goalkeeper's head for a spectacular goal!

"I've done it!" Yelled a thrilled McPlop.

"This is rigged!" Shouted Sidebottom.

McPlop quickly brought up the 'Cancel cheat' button and clicked it, to turn off the cheat in case Sidebottom got nosy. The substitute's rating changed back from 98 to 68.

"Phew!" Said McPlop and wiped his brow. "Just in the nick of time."

Sidebottom stuck his head around McPlop's door.

"This game is garbage, McPlop! It's clearly riddled with cheats."

"What are you talking about, Sidey? This is a brilliant game. Now go and sit yourself down and get ready for the referee's whistle to signal your imminent defeat."

Sidebottom stormed off back to his room and got the match underway.

"I'm going to check that substitute's rating." He clicked on the player's stats. "Hmmm, 68. Seems right. I don't understand why he's playing like a genius."

Another ten minutes of the match flew by with no further goals. The referee blew his whistle to signal a 2-1 win for McPlop's Manchester United team.

"Yesssssss!" Shouted McPlop and rushed round to stand in Sidebottom's doorway.

"We – are – topoftheleague, we – are - topoftheleague." McPlop chanted.

"I've had enough of this rubbish,

McPlop. I'm heading home."

"Yesssss! Sidebottom's quit! Result!" McPlop leapt up and down. "McPlop 'one', Sidebottom 'nil'." He said, beaming. "A famous victory for me today, young Sidebottom." McPlop added. "You might learn about how to mastermind victories like this one when you become a bit more experienced and a wiser manager, like myself, Sidey."

Sidebottom opened and closed his hand imitating McPlop's mouth yacking away. "Yeah, yeah, yeah. Do you know what I call it? I call it, 'McPlop-spawn'. Complete luck. Utter jam."

Sidebottom unplugged his controller and the pair walked downstairs to McPlop's hallway. Sidebottom put his shoes on and McPlop opened the front door for him.

"I think that was one of the most famous victories of all time." McPlop commented, as Sidebottom walked past him out of the front door.

"More like one of the biggest riggings

of all time, McPlop." Sidebottom replied. "The next session is at my house. You can't rig anything there."

McPlop gave him a huge grin.

"Bye Sidey." He said cheerily. "You might want to get a bit of practice in before our next session." He laughed as he watched Sidebottom disappear up the road muttering to himself about 'cheats' and 'riggings'.

8

The Cup Final Build Up

It was 5:30pm on a Wednesday afternoon and McPlop, who owned his own estate agency business, had finished his day's work. It had been a particularly good day as he had almost sold a house. Having locked the office up he was now whistling happily as he strolled home swinging his brief case as he walked.

On his way he passed a steady stream of people who were also heading home. He smiled and said, 'Hello' to each one of them as they passed, with some of them saying 'Hello' back and others just frowning at him as they thought he might be a bit odd.

Just then his phone started vibrating in his pocket.

"I've got a call!" He exclaimed loudly to everyone, which prompted funny looks from some passersby. McPlop fumbled in his pocket. The phone was blaring out the song, 'We Are the Champions' as its ring tone, which McPlop had downloaded to his phone after defeating Sidebottom at Fifa.

"It's an Unknown Number!" McPlop exclaimed excitedly, which drew more glances from the people walking towards him. He hit the green answer button and started speaking.

"You are through to McPlop's phone, there's no need to leave a message because it is I, the great McPlop, speaking to you, live!"

"McPlop, you idiot. It's me." Said Sidebottom, who was on the other end of the phone. "Now, listen up. We've both been invited to speak to the children at the local primary school to tell them about the Bob Poppleton Bakery Cup Final. We want as many people knowing about the final as possible, so we get a big crowd. What do you think? Do you want to join me, speaking to the kids? You can represent Spawn United and I'll tell them all about the great Sidebottom United."

"Of course, Sidey. Always happy to inspire the future generations with my wise words." McPlop replied. "When are we visiting the little darlings?"

"In two day's time, this Friday morning, in their assembly. I'll wear my Sidebottom United manager's tracksuit so they can see what a top-top-top manager looks like. You wear your Spawn United kit with the number nine on the back, so they can see what a top 'below-average' striker looks like.

"Top Bins!" Shouted McPlop into his mobile phone. "Count me in."

"Right, I'll call by your house on Friday morning before nine o'clock and we can wander up to the school." Sidebottom said and whacked the red button to finish the call.

Both the evening and the following day whizzed by and Friday's assembly came around very quickly. It would be starting in half an hour and McPlop was at home, waiting for Sidebottom to turn up at the end of his driveway.

McPlop had washed his Spawn United kit two days before but unfortunately had also put it into the tumble dryer, which resulted in his kit shrinking drastically. He had managed to just squeeze into it and was now standing in his bedroom in front of the mirror examining how he looked. His shirt was really tight around his gigantic belly, with his midriff on show. Although that wasn't quite how McPlop saw himself.

"Oh yes." Said McPlop, admiring his physique in the mirror as he turned from side to side. "Looking good, McPlop." He said, nodding at himself. He grabbed his phone and wallet and made his way downstairs and out of the front door. Waiting at the top of his driveway was Sidebottom, dressed in his Sidebottom United tracksuit, wearing two Sidebottom United scarves and carrying a couple of Sidebottom United mugs.

He looked at McPlop whose football kit was skin-tight, making McPlop's belly look huge.

"When's your baby due?" Asked Sidebottom and then started laughing at his own joke.

"Yes, very witty, Sidebottom. I just had a mishap with the tumble dryer, that's all." McPlop explained. "Right, we'd better go or we'll be late."

In the main hall of the school all the children were sitting in rows looking up at the stage where the headteacher, Mr Bumfluff, had just finished handing out the 'Stars of the week' and 'Stars of the lunchtime' awards. The children who had been standing near the headteacher with their certificates had all been holding their noses because the headteacher was a bit smelly hence the nickname they all gave him of, 'Smelly Bumfluff'.

"Now children," said Smelly Bumfluff, "it gives me great pleasure to introduce you to two men who will be competing against each other in a football cup final this weekend." The headteacher, who had a particularly bad memory was frantically trying to recall the name of the cup competition. "The men are competing in the um…the um….Billy Bottle-it cup final?" He looked over at Sidebottom to see if he had got the name right. Sidebottom had his head in his hands. The headteacher decided to try and get the pair onto the stage as soon as possible.

"So, children, please give a warm welcome to um….to um…wait I know it…I know it… Mr Ploppy McBottom and Mr Sidepoop?" He looked over to the two football men to see if he had got their names right. Sidebottom had slapped his own forehead in dismay whilst McPlop was chuckling away to himself.

The headteacher waved to the men to get them onto the stage and departed down the steps at the other side.

Sidebottom and McPlop looked at each other to see who was going up onto the stage first.

"After you, Sidepoop." McPlop said and started laughing.

"Watch it, McBottom." Sidebottom replied and walked up the steps onto the stage with McPlop following behind.

"Good morning children, I'm Mr Sidebottom. I'm the manager of Sidebottom United and my players sometimes call me 'boss' or 'gaffer' and I'm sure I've heard them also call me 'governor', 'main man', 'top dog', 'number one', 'your lordship' or even 'your imperial greatness'.

McPlop was frowning quizzically as he turned his head slowly round to look at Sidebottom. He had never heard any of Sidebottom's players calling him by those names. The only names he'd heard the players call him were 'The Butt' and the 'The Royal doofuss'.

Sidebottom looked at all the children who seemed to be listening very intently to what he was saying, "This weekend, boys and girls, is a colossal match between the big guns, Sidebottom United,

Hurrah!" Sidebottom punched the air to try and get the kids to cheer for his team, "and minnows, Spawn United. Booooo!" Said Sidebottom using his hands as a funnel to make the booing louder.

"Minnows! Pah!" Spluttered McPlop. "We're going to thrash you, Sidebottom. Remember our team has got 'spawn' on its side."

"Oh yeah," replied Sidebottom, trying to think of a quick response, "well our team's got bottom on its side."

"That doesn't even make sense!" Replied McPlop.

"Either way, your team's going down, McPoop."

The kids chuckled.

"Urm, thank you for that, gentlemen." The headteacher, Mr Bumfuff said, interrupting their presentation before it turned into an argument.

"Urr, I've not finished yet, Bumfluff." Said Sidebottom indignantly.

"I beg your pardon! You should refer to me as MISTER Bumfluff."

"But I thought your name was Bertie Bumfluff?" Challenged McPlop.

All the children started laughing, now they had found out the headteacher's real name.

"Right, you two, get off the stage now." Ordered Smelly Bumfluff.

The pair hurried off and went down the steps at the other side, with Sidebottom shouting, "The cup final's at three o'clock tomorrow afternoon and any children coming along to support Sidebottom United will get a free Sidebottom United mug! Hurrah!" Sidebottom punched the air again.

"Never mind trying to flog your cheap mugs, you two," shouted Bertie Bumfluff, "get out of my school!"

The children watched as the pair ran past them towards the doors.

"Yo, bumfluff!" Shouted Sidebottom at the headteacher as he ran, "don't forget to take a shower!"

9

The Cup Final

The following day, McPlop, who had gone to bed very late, woke from his slumber. It took him a few seconds to realise what day it was.

"It's Saturday. Cup final day!" He exclaimed and leapt out of bed. He started jumping up and down and flapping his arms around as a vague attempt at exercise. He then started doing star jumps, followed by some pretend boxing.

He looked at his clock.

"11:38am!" He shrieked. "The match kicks off in twenty two minutes!" He glanced at his phone.

"Thirty two answerphone messages!" He exclaimed. "Oops, they're all from the Spawn United manager."

McPlop listened to the most recent one.

"GET HERE NOW, MCPLOP!" Was

the message his manager had screamed into the phone a few minutes before.

McPlop hurriedly got his Spawn United kit on. Despite the rush he was very excited. The chance to play against Sidebottom United in the cup final! More importantly the chance to beat Sidebottom's team in the final! McPlop couldn't contain himself.

"This is so exciting!" He said as he pulled his football boots on, grabbed a slice of cold pizza that he had left over from the previous night and ran out of the door.

It had just passed noon and I was looking at my watch and put my referee's whistle to my mouth, ready to signal the start of the cup final.

I had delayed as long as possible to allow McPlop to get here for the kick off. I put my red and yellow cards into the back pocket of my referee's shorts. Just as I was about to blow the whistle, McPlop came half running, half staggering round the corner, panting heavily.

"I'm ready," He said, then doubled over and gulped in some air. "It's okay, I'm here."

"Thank goodness for that." Shouted the Spawn United manager, who now had his full first team.

"Thank goodness for that." Shouted Sidebottom, who was getting worried that Spawn United were about to put a decent striker up front instead of McPlop.

As McPlop walked onto the pitch I signaled to the two keepers to ensure they were ready and then blew the whistle.

Within seconds Sidebottom United player Francesco Piddle was launching into tackles and the Spawn United players were having to jump out of his way to avoid being scythed down.

One of the Spawn United midfielders saw Piddle hurtling towards him, so decided to get rid of the ball as quickly as possible.

"Here, McPlop!" He shouted and kicked the ball into his teammate's path.

Piddle galloped round the midfielder and went charging towards McPlop. Anticipating that McPlop would get to the ball before him, Piddle slid both feet forwards towards the ball in a dangerous sliding tackle. McPlop however was so slow that he hadn't got near the ball and Piddle missed McPlop completely. McPlop then slipped over, trying to stay out of Piddle's way and landed on the turf. He started waving his arms around.

"Foul, referee! VAR! VAR!"

"What are you talking about, McPlop?" Yelled Sidebottom from the touchline.

"VAR!" Shouted McPlop, in my direction. He had now got up from the ground and was using his fingers to make a TV screen shape in mid-air. "VAR, referee!"

"McPlop, you complete buffon. Stop shouting VAR at everyone." Shouted Sidebottom. "How on earth can there be VAR when we're in the middle of a field and there are no cameras. This isn't the Premier League!"

"Ref-er-ee!" Shouted McPlop and threw some mud down to the ground.

"Pipe down, McPlop." I commented as I walked towards him. "Piddle didn't even touch you. Just because Spawn United have paid two tracksuits for you, doesn't mean you can start acting like billy-big-time."

McPlop could see he wasn't going to get a free kick, so sloped away and headed to an area well away from the crazy Francesco Piddle.

Ten minutes later and the score was still 0-0 in the cup final with the only incident of note being when I had booked Piddle for booting the ball at his own manager, Sidebottom, who had been moaning at him.

A few minutes later McPlop was standing waiting for a corner to come in when Piddle bumped into McPlop as he was waddling towards the ball. McPlop paused for a second then did a huge dive and subsequently rolled over five times.

Eventually he rolled right up to where I was standing. He then paused for dramatic effect and promptly rolled all the way back to where the foul took place. I shook my head at McPlop's antics but put my whistle to my mouth and pointed to the penalty spot.

"Penalty!" I announced.

"That was never a penalty referee!" Shouted Sidebottom, who was leaping up and down in fury. "You're blind ref!" Sidebottom then turned to two old ladies who were walking past the football pitch talking about knitting and not paying any attention to the football. "Did you see that?" Sidebottom said. "That was a disgrace! Piddle barely touched him." The two old ladies had no idea who this 'Piddle' person was, so shrugged their shoulders and carried on their conversations about knitting patterns. It was now McPlop's turn to see if he could get even more than a penalty.

"Yellow card for Piddle, referee, surely!" Shouted McPlop, who had now got up from the ground and was waving an imaginary yellow card in my direction.

"Yes, thank you, McPlop. I'm quite capable of refereeing this match myself. I don't need your input." I pulled out my yellow card and booked McPlop as he wasn't allowed to try and get another player booked.

"Good decision referee!" Shouted Sidebottom from behind me. "You're an excellent ref!"

I then turned to Francesco Piddle and called him over. I reached into my back pocket and showed him first a yellow card for the foul, followed by a red card as this was his second booking.

"A red card!" Screamed Sidebottom. "You're a disgrace referee! You need your head examining!"

Piddle trudged off the pitch. Once he had gone I marched over to where Sidebottom was standing on the touchline.

"Right, I've heard enough from you as well, Sidebottom." I put the red card in front of his face and pointed over towards the pavilion. "You're sent off as well."

"Ref-er-ee." Said a deflated Sidebottom who turned away in a resigned manner and threw his water bottle down to the ground. He trailed after Piddle to the pavilion.

Meanwhile an excited McPlop had placed the ball on the penalty spot and glanced over in my direction to see if he was allowed to take the penalty kick yet.

I blew my whistle and McPlop ran up to the ball. He toe-punted it as hard as he could and the ball went rocketing past the keeper and into the net.

"Yesssss!" The Spawn United players screamed. All the players jumped on top of McPlop in celebration. The score now read:

Spawn United 1-0 Sidebottom United
(McPlop)

As the first half drew to a close I blew my whistle and the players all made their way over to the two dugouts for the half-time break.

A humble Sidebottom came walking over from the pavillion to speak to me.

"Apologies, Mr Langley. I might have got a little carried away earlier. You have to understand that this is the Bob Poppleton Bakery Cup Final. It's the biggest match of any young manager's career." He bowed his head. "I wondered if you might let me back into the dug out for the second half. I need to be able to make substitutions which I can't do from the pavillion."

"Hmmm." I paused, thinking about it. "Yes, I suppose you do need to be able to make subs. Okay, you can come back but I don't want to hear another squeak out of you."

"He shoots, he scores!" Shouted Sidebottom and punched the air. "I'm back in the game!"

I rolled my eyes and wandered away.

About mid-way through the second half Sidebottom was getting increasingly agitated on the touchline. Worse still was that McPlop had moved over to the same wing and was positioned in front of him.

"What's the score, Sidey?" McPlop whispered and started chuckling.

"You just wait, McPlop. It's not finished yet."

Sidebottom United had started to get on top and were attacking, with most of the Spawn United players back defending. Only McPlop had remained up front. Suddenly the ball was cleared upfield out to the wing where McPlop was standing. He set off running virtually along the touchline. Sidebottom watched him coming up the line towards him.

"Referee! Look at that helicopter behind you!" Shouted Sidebottom and pointed past me. I turned around to look at what Sidebottom was shouting about, just as McPlop was running past Sidebottom on the touchline. Sidebottom stuck a foot out, McPlop tripped over it and went flying, landing on his belly in a puddle.

"Ref-er-ee!" McPlop screamed. "Their

manager just tripped me up!" He yelled and pointed at Sidebottom, who had stepped a couple of strides back from the touchline.

"What, referee?" Sidebottom held his arms out to his side, his face a picture of innocence. "I was nowhere near him! He just fell over."

"I didn't see it, McPlop." I shouted. "We'll have to play on. That's a Sidebottom United throw-in. It must have come off you, McPlop."

"Substitution referee!" Shouted Sidebottom, before McPlop could complain about my decision.

I blew the whistle to stop the players playing on, then watched as Sidebottom took his tracksuit top off to reveal his Sidebottom United kit.

"I'm bringing myself on." The manager announced. "I'm registered as player-manager." He was now furiously trying to get his trouser bottoms off.

"Get on with it then, Sidebottom." I said, as the player-manager got his foot stuck in one of the trouser legs and then tumbled over. Eventually he got the trousers off and jogged on to replace one of his players.

Play continued until the ninetieth minute, with Spawn United still winning 1-0.

"Three minutes injury time to play." I shouted to the players.

Could Spawn United hold on for a famous win?

Would they beat Sidebottom United and win the cup?

Or could the player-manager, Sidebottom, get an equaliser for ten-man Sidebottom United and take the cup final to extra-time?

The first thing Sidebottom was going to have to do was defend though because Spawn United were on the attack. The ball deflected off a Sidebottom United player for a corner. The Spawn United winger jogged over, placed the ball by the corner flag and then crossed the ball in. It was arrowing towards McPlop. McPlop swung a foot at the ball, connected with it but the ball shot off in the wrong direction, whacked against Sidebottom's head which then diverted the ball back in the direction of the Sidebottom United goal. The stunned keeper could only stand and watch in surprise as he was totally wrong-footed. The ball flew past him into the goal!

"2-0!" Screamed the Spawn United players in joy.

"We've surely won the cup now!" Shouted McPlop, who punched the air.

"Cracking own goal from Sidebottom!" Yelled another player who then ran past Sidebottom, patted him on the back and said, "Nice finish."

The Spawn United manager, who had been quite reserved until now came running onto the pitch.

"McPlop's done it again!" He ran over and hugged McPlop. "That's the best two tracksuits I've ever spent! A goal and an assist in the Bob Poppleton Bakery Cup Final. That's quite incredible." The Spawn United manager was jumping up and down and I had to usher him off the pitch so we could play the last couple of minutes of the match.

The game petered out and eventually I blew the whistle.

Final Score:

The Bob Poppleton Bakery Cup Final

Spawn United 2-0 Sidebottom United
(McPlop, Sidebottom o.g)

Man of the match:
'Two Tracksuits' McPlop

10

The Presentation

The players all headed back to the changing rooms as they needed to get washed and dressed ready for the presentation of the much heralded Bob Poppleton Bakery Cup Trophy.

The two changing rooms were either side of a huge communal bath for the players. It was an old fashioned tiled bath that was so big about twenty players could bathe in it at the same time. There were currently about fifteen people in the huge bath all getting washed.

All of a sudden the door burst open and Francesco Piddle stood there stripped and ready for the bath. Instead of climbing in carefully though, he took a running leap, jumped as high as he could towards the middle of the bath and landed with a huge splash in the middle of all the bathers. Water went everywhere, all over everyone's shoes that were just outside the bath.

"Francesco, you buffoon!" Yelled Sidebottom, who was one of the people in the huge communal bath.

"Hey lads, check this out." Said Piddle, after he surfaced. He then frowned and concentrated really hard, then let out an underwater trump for about five seconds. It made a huge sound and then loads of bubbles rose to the surface of the bath. All the other players froze for a second as they realised how bad this was going to smell. Then each of them started shouting.

"Everyone out! Piddle's let one rip." Screamed one player.

"This'll be a right stinker. Save yourselves!" Shouted a second player.

"Get the heck out of here!" Yelled another.

"Every man for himself," shouted a fourth and used his hand to push back an opposition player so he could get out of the bath quicker.

"Noooo, not the bubbles!" Shouted the player who fell back into the bubbles that surrounded Francesco Piddle.

"Breathe it in boys!" Grinned Francesco. "Gotta love that aroma." He shouted as he laughed hysterically.

The players scrambled over one another to escape until the only person left in the bath was Piddle.

He sat back and relaxed into one of the underwater seats.

Not long after, everyone had got changed into their clothes and they left the changing rooms to go back onto the pitch where Bob Poppleton himself was standing next to a huge silver cup.

"Gather round lads." Bob said to the players.

"Now, it gives me great pleasure to award the Bob Poppleton trophy to Spawn United!" There was a ripple of applause from all the Sidebottom United players except for one shout from the back from Sidebottom.

"It was a fix." He shouted and then pointed at someone else to try and make out that it was them who had shouted.

Bob Poppleton ignored him.

"Now, if the manager of Spawn United and also their star striker, McPlop would like to come up, they can collect the trophy."

The pair walked over, shook hands with Bob Poppleton and then carefully lifted the cup above their heads, to cheers from all the Spawn United players.

"We did it, McPlop!" Said the Spawn United manager as he hugged his star striker. McPlop then decided he would say a few words.

"Firstly well done to all of the Spawn United players. Secondly I owe a lot to my former manager, Sidebottom, who started me off on this road to stardom." Sidebottom rolled his eyes, as McPlop continued. "I've known old Sidey for a number of years now and for those of you who don't know him, let me tell you something about my friend. He's a difficult man to ignore…but do try, because it's well worth the effort…"

Children's Books by Adrian Lobley

Sidebottom & McPlop
Children's Humour (ages 7-11)

Kane series
Football (Historical) fiction

The Football Maths Book series
Books that use fun football puzzles to help children with maths (ages 4-9)

A Learn to Read Book series
Books that use football and tennis to help children read their first words (ages 4-5 years)

For more information visit: www.adrianlobley.com

Printed in Great Britain
by Amazon

83746227R00078